2017

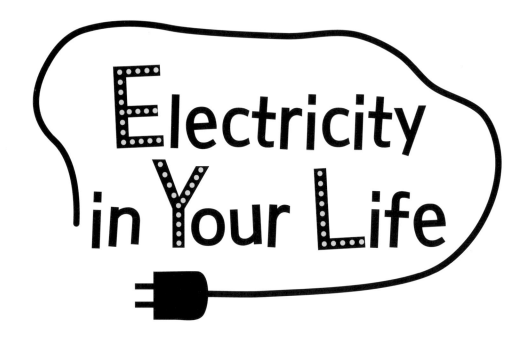

Electricity in Your Life

Written by Bo-hyun Seo   Illustrated by Sung-hwa Kwak

TanTan Publishing

Turn on the television, enjoy some toast with strawberry jam, and watch funny cartoons.

Lights, refrigerator, toaster, TV.
These devices all use electricity.
There are many electrical devices
around us.

We eat to get energy.
We need energy to live.

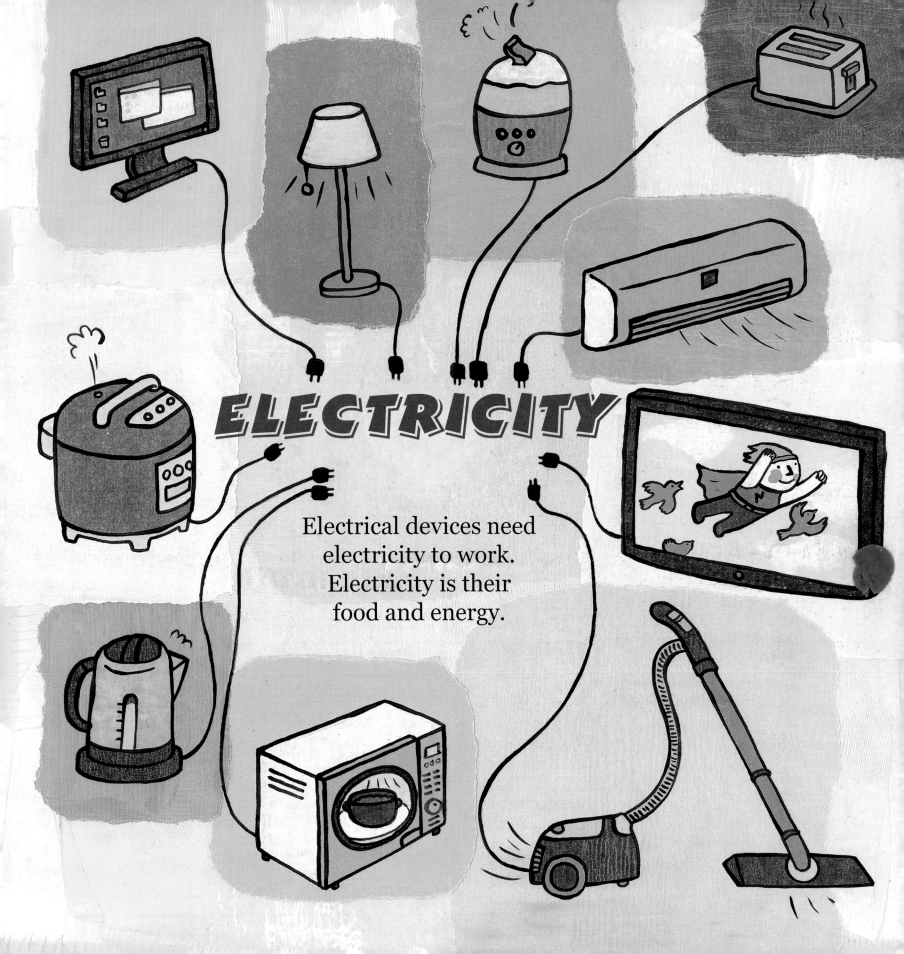

ELECTRICITY

Electrical devices need electricity to work. Electricity is their food and energy.

Electricity goes into electrical devices and does many things.
It can shine a bright light.
It can generate warm heat.
It can make machines buzz like a bee.

Electricity is generated at a power plant.
At power plants you can see huge waterfalls
that generate hydropower,
howling winds for wind power,
and scorching sunlight for solar power,
These all have a lot of energy that can be used
to make electricity.

A long and lengthy wire.

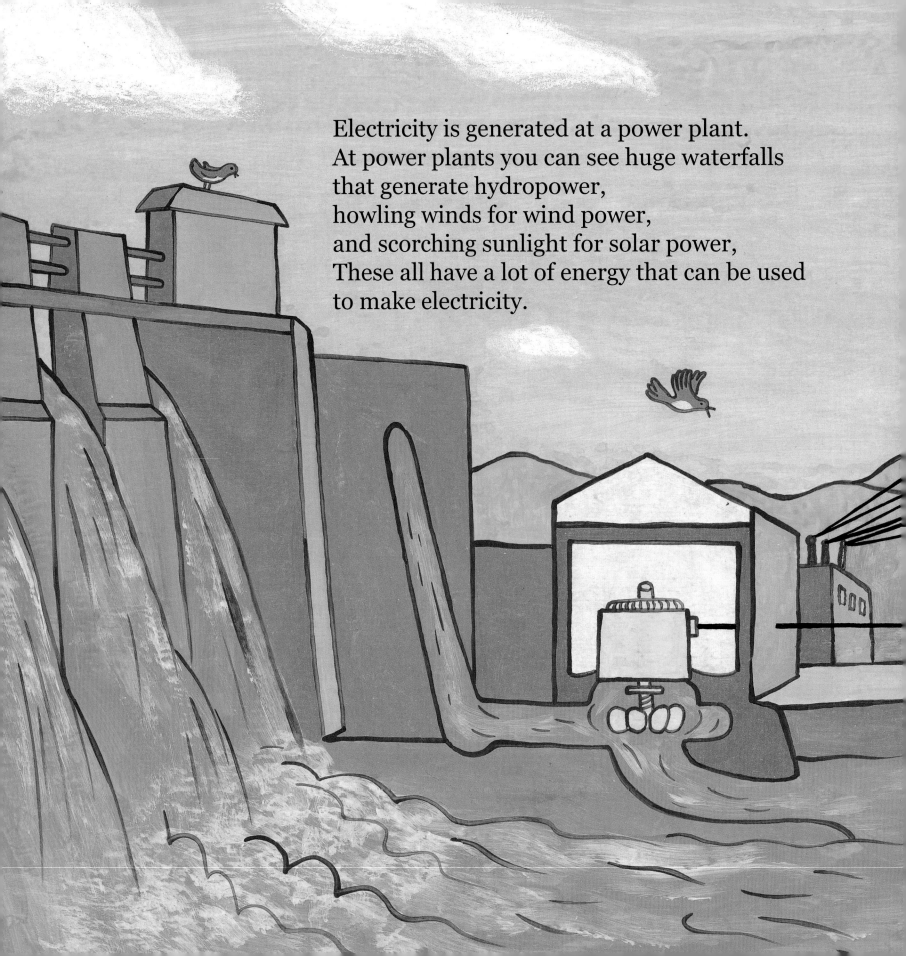

Electricity is generated at a power plant.
At power plants you can see huge waterfalls
that generate hydropower,
howling winds for wind power,
and scorching sunlight for solar power,
These all have a lot of energy that can be used
to make electricity.

Electricity from the power plant travels through large wires.
These wires are like roads for electricity.
Electricity travels through wires on telephone poles,
or passes through underground tubes, and keeps on going to...

... hospitals, department stores, factories, subways, or my house. Electricity can travel anywhere through electric wires.

Anywhere electricity travels,
there are always electric wires.
If you cannot see the electric wires,
they are hidden in the walls or in the ground.
When electric wires are disconnected,
there is no electricity.

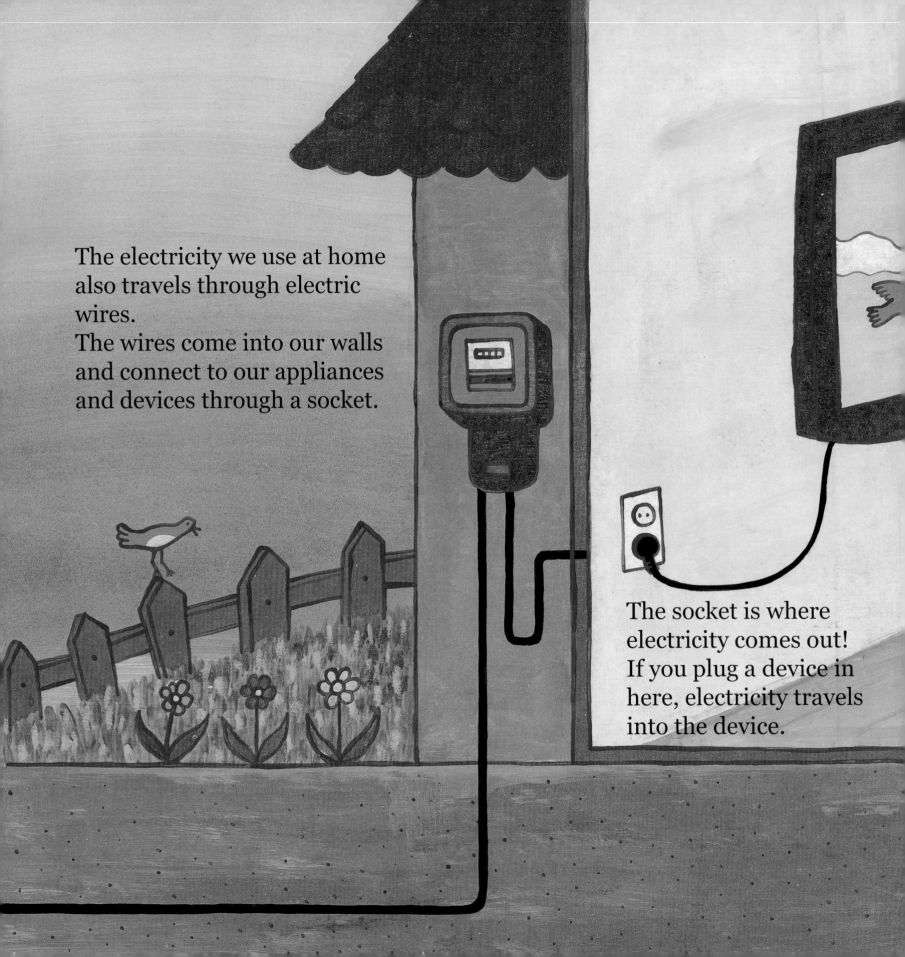

The electricity we use at home also travels through electric wires.
The wires come into our walls and connect to our appliances and devices through a socket.

The socket is where electricity comes out! If you plug a device in here, electricity travels into the device.

After you plug the device into the socket, turn on the switch. The electrical device is working!

The elevator wasn't working, so I had to walk up 15 floors.
APT 106
The computer is not working, so I can't do my homework or play any games.

The lights are back on!
We have electricity again!

Thank you, electricity! We will use it well!

First, we should save electricity:
It takes a lot of energy to make electricity so we need to use it wisely.

Use devices that consume less electricity.

Unplug devices when they're not being used.

Second, be careful:
Electricity can be very dangerous.

Do not touch electrical devices with wet hands.

Do not insert anything into the socket.

End of electricity story!

Battery Story

Batteries are small containers with electricity stored inside.

You don't need to plug a battery into a socket, but you can still use the electricity. This makes it possible to take devices with you. Devices that use batteries for electricity, like flashlights, radios or cameras, have a place inside to hold them. When you use up all the electricity in the batteries, make sure you throw them into the recycle bin!

About the Author
Bo-hyun Seo received a Master's in Child Studies at Yonsei University. She has written *The Anchovy's Dream, Why Do We Bleed When We Fall Down?*, *Mr. Parkrooge's Christmas, I Am The Longest*, and many others.

About the Illustrator
Sung-hwa Kwak studied visual design in college and completed the Illustration program at Hangook Illustration School. Her work includes *Korean, A Bowl that Contains Our Language, Don't Tell Anyone, The Boy With Flags of All Nations* and many others.

Tantan Publishing Knowledge Storybook *Electricity in Your Life*

www.TantanPublishing.com

Published in the U.S. in 2016 by TANTAN PUBLISHING, INC.
4005 w Olympic Blvd., Los Angeles, CA 90019-3258

©Copyright 2016 by Dong-hwi Kim
English Edition

ISBN: 978-1-939248-16-9

Printed in Korea